Whale Rescue

written by Pam Holden
illustrated by Lamia Aziz

Baby Whale lived with his family far out in the deep sea. One morning, he swam away all by himself. Before long, he knew that he was lost. He felt frightened because he couldn't see any of the other whales.

aby Whale swam a long way as he tried to find his
amily. After a while, he swam too close to the beach.
he water at the beach was not deep enough for a
hale! First he tried to swim forwards and then he
ried to swim backwards.

Soon Baby Whale knew he was stuck in the soft sand. He flapped his tail hard and he shook his flippers, but he couldn't swim at all because the water was too shallow. He felt very frightened and worried.

Who will save me?" he cried. "Please help me!"
he big whales were trying to find their lost baby.
Vhen they heard his cries, they swam quickly through
he waves to the beach to help him.

The two big whales swam closer and closer to the beach, but they were far too big to swim in such shallow water. Before long, they were both stuck in the soft sand, too.

A family playing on the beach saw the whales splashing
n the waves, flapping their tails and trying to swim.
"Don't worry! We'll help you," the people shouted, as
hey ran quickly into the water.

"The water isn't deep enough here for the whales to swim away," the people said to each other. "We'll have to wait for the tide to come right in. The water will get deeper soon."

/hile they waited, they put wet towels
n the whales' backs to keep them cool. The children
ound pieces of seaweed in the waves. They put it
n the whales' heads to keep the sun off their skin.

The people filled their buckets with cool sea water and they poured it gently all over the whales' backs to keep them wet.

'hey patted the three whales and talked to them to ıake them feel better. "We'll look after you," they aid. "Don't worry. The tide is coming back in now."

Slowly the water at the beach got deeper and deeper. After a while, the children gave Baby Whale a hard push, and he tried to swim by himself.

e flapped his tail and his flippers, while the children ushed him harder and harder. Slowly he swam away om the beach into deeper water.

As soon as the water was deep enough, the people pushed the big whales out through the waves, too. "You're safe now! Goodbye!" they shouted, as the whales began to swim by themselves.

hey were so happy to be back in the deep water
gain that they dived and jumped and splashed.
he people watched as the whales waved their tails
o say, "Thank you for saving us!"

The people were very pleased too.
"Goodbye, Whale Family," they shouted.
"Remember to stay out there in the deep sea.
Don't ever swim close to the beach again!"